Nikki & Deja

ELECTION MADNESS

by Karen English

Illustrated by Laura Freeman

Clarion Books
Houghton Mifflin Harcourt
Boston ★ New York
2011

To all the Nikkis and Dejas everywhere
—K.E.

For Roberta
—L.F.

Clarion Books
215 Park Avenue South
New York, New York 10003

Text copyright © 2011 by Karen English
Illustrations copyright © 2011 by Laura Freeman

The text of this book is set in 13.5 Warnock Pro.
The illustrations were executed digitally.

For information about permission to reproduce selections from this book,
write to Permissions, Houghton Mifflin Harcourt Publishing Company,
215 Park Avenue South, New York, New York 10003.

Clarion Books is an imprint of Houghton Mifflin Harcourt
Publishing Company.

www.hmhbooks.com

Library of Congress Cataloging-in-Publication Data
English, Karen.
Nikki and Deja : election madness / by Karen English ; illustrated by Laura Freeman.
p. cm.
Summary: When Carver Elementary holds school-wide elections for the first time,
third-grader Deja puts all her efforts into running for school president, ignoring her
best friend Nikki's problems.
ISBN 978-0-547-43558-9
[1. Politics, Practical—Fiction. 2. Elections—Fiction. 3. Schools—Fiction.
4. Best friends—Fiction. 5. Friendship—Fiction. 6. African Americans—Fiction.]
I. Freeman-Hines, Laura, ill.
II. Title. III. Title: Election madness.
PZ7.E7232Nim 2011
[Fic]—dc22
2011008151

Manufactured in the United States of America
DOC 10 9 8 7 6 5 4 3 2 1
4500297718

– Contents –

1

You're Not
the Boss of Me

Nikki isn't playing right. She's holding her paddle wrong and she isn't keeping her eye on the ball. Plus she's hitting too hard and the Ping-Pong ball isn't even bouncing on the table. Deja has to keep chasing it and she's getting tired.

"You're hitting the ball too hard."

"Am not."

"Yeah, you are." Deja lobs an easy one to her. Nikki completely misses it.

"You have to keep your eye on the ball, Nikki."

Nikki doesn't say anything. She just digs around in the bushes behind her. She throws the ball hard back to Deja so she can serve again. It sails softly over the table and lands right in Deja's hand. Nikki looks disappointed.

Deja hits the next ball lightly, right at Nikki, as if she were five years old and Deja was teaching her how to play Ping-Pong by going very, very easy. Nikki watches it bounce, then doesn't even trouble herself, it seems to Deja, to reach for it. She deliberately lets the ball bounce twice before she swings at it and misses.

Deja is exasperated. "You can't let the ball bounce twice, Nikki. It can only bounce once. And you're not even trying!"

"Be quiet!" Nikki shouts. "You're not the boss of me!"

Deja puts her paddle down. "What's wrong with you?"

"Nothing! I'm just getting tired of you bossing me around."

"I'm not even bossing you around! I'm just trying to tell you how to play."

Nikki's face is scrunched so that her eyebrows jut up on the ends like a Halloween mask. Her mouth turns down as if she is about to cry. Then she does cry. She slams the paddle on the ground and stomps off to the porch steps. She flings herself down and puts her face in her hands.

Deja checks to see if her brand-new paddle is harmed in any way, then marches over to Nikki.

Auntie Dee and her friend Phoebe had spent

the morning setting up the Ping-Pong table, first on the grass because there was more shade, then in front of the garage, where there was cement. Auntie Dee had thought the grassy spot under the tree was better because it would be cooler, but then she changed her mind and thought the table would be sturdier if it was on a hard surface. Finally, it was set up. It was Auntie's way of giving Deja more to do outside—away from too much TV.

"What's the matter with you?" Deja asks again, when she's settled next to Nikki on the steps. Nikki's nose is running. She reaches up and wipes it with the heel of her hand, then runs her hand over her pant leg to clean off the snot. She sniffs loudly.

"Nothing," Nikki answers quietly. "I just don't like being bossed."

"But nobody's gonna cry over that, Nikki. Tell me the truth."

Nikki looks like she's trying to make up her mind whether to tell Deja what's really going on.

She drops her face into her arms, resting on bent knees. Deja hears her mumble something, but she can't make out what it is.

"What? I can't understand what you're saying."

Nikki mumbles something again. Deja strains hard to make out the words, but she simply can't.

"Put your head up, Nikki, so I can hear you."

Nikki raises her head and from her quivering mouth come the words "I think my mom and dad are getting a divorce."

"What?" Deja wonders if she heard her correctly. She couldn't possibly have said what she thinks she said. "They're getting a *divorce?*" Deja blurts out.

"I said I *think* they're getting a divorce. They had a big argument on Tuesday and they haven't spoken to each other since." She looks over at Deja, her face smeared with tears, and takes in a shuddery breath. "They keep talking to each other through me! And I don't like it!"

Deja doesn't know what to say. She doesn't even know what expression to put on her face. "Just because they're not speaking doesn't mean they're getting divorced. People stop speaking to each other all the time." The words sound truer to Deja as she goes along. "Auntie Dee and her friend Phoebe stopped speaking for a long time once."

Nikki wipes her eyes, and when her hands come away, she looks hopeful. "When was that?" she asks.

The trouble is, Deja doesn't remember when it was. And maybe she exaggerated about it being a long time . . . but she likes the look on Nikki's face.

"What was it about?" Nikki presses.

Deja is trying to think of something to say when Auntie Dee sticks her head out the door and calls, "Who wants to go to the mall?"

"We do," Nikki and Deja say together, and Nikki jumps up to run next door to her own house to get permission.

Auntie Dee has picked up her friend Phoebe, even though she just lives across the street and down some. Now they are headed for the mall.

In the back seat of the car, Nikki whispers to Deja, "How much money do you have?"

"How much do you have?" Deja replies, wondering if Nikki is getting ready to ask her for some of her money.

"Two dollars."

"Oh, I have five."

Nikki looks out the window as if she's thinking about this. Then she whispers, "Do you think your auntie will let us go to the Candy Palace?"

"I'll ask." Deja knows she has to handle this just right. Auntie is a vegetarian and only eats organic stuff. She makes Deja eat all kinds of healthy meals and snacks. Getting permission to go to the Candy Palace is going to be tricky. Nikki looks over at Deja expectantly, but Deja just stares out the window. It's better to wait.

"Don't wander off," Auntie Dee says as they go through the heavy doors at the mall entrance. That means they have to follow Auntie and Phoebe into Lily's Shoes and watch while Phoebe tries on one pair after another.

Finally, they get to leave that store and move on to the next. Phoebe's still looking for shoes. Auntie's giving her advice and looking for a new bag while she's at it. Deja can already tell this is not going to be fun. The one good thing is that they're moving in the direction of the Candy Palace. She can see the words *Candy Palace* lit up in tiny rainbow-colored lights. Who could resist wandering in there?

Auntie Dee and Phoebe are walking at a brisk pace. If Deja doesn't make her move, they're bound to pass right by the shop and all its heavenly confections. "Auntie Dee . . ." She puts just the right amount of whine in her voice.

"What is it?" Something has caught Auntie's eye on the other side of the walkway. She's elbowing Phoebe and they're about to cross.

"Can we go look in the Candy Palace?" Deja blurts. "Puhleeze . . ."

Auntie Dee sighs. She twists her mouth, thinking. Deja holds her breath. She can feel Nikki holding her breath as well. "All right. You can buy *one* thing. I mean it—*one thing*. But you can't eat it until after you've had your dinner."

This is not exactly what Deja had in mind. She can't help but frown a little. She's just about to protest when she catches Nikki's excited smile. She knows Nikki's already thinking of the sour sugar whips and the gummy balls and the whirly suckers. Deja's mouth begins to water. She'll promise anything for the chance to go into the Candy Palace. "Okay, okay," she says with growing anticipation.

"Phoebe and I are just going to check that shoe store across the way. As soon as you get your *one thing* I want you to come directly there to meet us. Do you understand?"

"Yes, Auntie Dee."

Auntie Dee and Phoebe head to the shoe store, and Nikki and Deja turn in to the Candy Palace.

There's so much to choose from, but they have their favorites. Deja's mouth waters again at the sight of the cherry sour whips crammed in their plastic case, the sugar granules glittering under the store lights. Nikki pauses in front of a case filled with hot cinnamon suckers. Deja sees her swallow. Slowly they walk along, scanning the walls that are covered floor to ceiling with displays. While the clerk waits on a slowly deciding older lady, they scrutinize the candy-filled cases. Deja doesn't want to make her decision too hurriedly. Perhaps there's something she might like better than sour whips and hot cinnamon lollipops.

"May I help you?" the clerk finally asks. He's tall and skinny with pimples on his forehead. He looks tired even though it's still morning.

Deja moves to the counter. "Nikki, come here." Nikki is still staring at things on the wall.

"I'm not finished looking," she protests.

"Come on, Nikki. You know what you always get." Deja turns back to the clerk. "I want five hot cinnamon suckers, five sour whips— cherry—and, um . . ." It's hard for Deja to decide what else she wants to spend her money on. She scans the case in front of her. Everything looks so good.

"Auntie Dee said one thing, Deja," Nikki reminds her.

"I know what she said."

"Well, you're getting more than one thing," Nikki says, and Deja doesn't like the goody-good tone in her voice.

"I'm only going to eat one thing today, one thing tomorrow, and one thing the next day," Deja explains.

Nikki narrows her eyes. "Your auntie is going to be really mad, Deja, when she sees all that candy."

"You can keep it for me at your house and then I'll just get one thing a day."

"I don't know . . ."

"Come on, Nikki."

"But then she'll see me with a big bag of

candy, and she might tell my mom, and then I'll get in trouble."

"Gosh, Nikki, don't be such a baby." Deja pays for her selections and the clerk hands her a bag stuffed full.

"Your turn," the clerk says to Nikki, yawning.

"I want a hot cinnamon sucker," Nikki says, "and two cherry sour whips."

"That's what I'm getting," Deja says. "Get something else, so we can share. Get the chocolate spiders."

"I don't want the chocolate spiders. I want what I said."

"But we can share them. I can give you a cherry sour whip and you can give me some chocolate spiders—like that."

Nikki turns toward Deja then, and her lip quivers as she says loudly, "Be quiet, Deja. Quit bossing me around. You're not the boss of me!"

Ms. Shelby's Good News

At school the next morning, Ms. Shelby looks like she has a delicious secret. The way her lips are pressed together in a puckery little smile makes Deja imagine that she's sucking on a butter toffee. They are just about to go out for morning recess. Ms. Shelby stands with her back to the whiteboard and her hands folded in front of her.

"I have some good news," she says. Everyone looks her way to see what she's going to say. "But you're going to have to wait to find out what it is. By the time you go home today, you'll know what my surprise is."

The class exits slowly. Nikki and Deja spend recess guessing what the good news could be.

"Ms. Shelby is engaged," Nikki says as soon as they reach the handball court.

"No," Deja says. "That can't be it. She doesn't even have a ring on her finger. I think we're going on a field trip. We've only been on one to Riley Farms. And that was spoiled when Howard threw up and stunk up the bus the whole way back."

Nikki wrinkles her nose, remembering.

"Maybe we're going to the aquarium," Deja continues. She takes a hot cinnamon sucker out of her pocket, looks around, and then unwraps it.

Nikki's eyes widen. "Deja, you're going to get in trouble. We're not supposed to have candy at school."

"I'm only taking a couple of licks." She takes two licks, then wraps it up again and puts it back in her pocket. Nikki looks relieved.

By the middle of the day, Ms. Shelby's surprise is almost forgotten. The class walks in from lunch recess, hot and sweaty and ready to listen to the latest installment of *The Whipping Boy*. They're allowed to put their heads down on their desks and even close their eyes while Ms. Shelby reads. Deja especially likes *The Whipping Boy* because it began with the theme of getting whipped for bad behavior. She's growing a little disappointed with the direction the story is taking, though. She doesn't like that the naughty prince gets to escape his punishment and the poor whipping boy must take his place. It's not as much fun, she thinks, as seeing the prince get what he deserves.

Deja is all ready to take her seat and put her head down when Ms. Shelby reminds them about her good news. Deja sits up and yawns. She looks over at Nikki. Nikki's leaning forward a little bit in her chair, smiling as if she already knows what Ms. Shelby is going to say.

"What do you think my big surprise is?"

Hands fly up. Ms. Shelby looks around. She points to Howard.

"Pizza party?" he asks. Deja looks at him, annoyed. What have they done to earn a pizza party? Nothing.

"No, not a pizza party. Alyssa?" Ms. Shelby asks, moving on.

Everyone turns to Alyssa. She smiles. The class waits. She brings her chin down and stares at her desk, still smiling.

"Remember," Ms. Shelby says, "only raise your hand when you have something to say." Finally, she looks in Deja's direction. Deja waves her hand and rises a bit out of her seat, but then sits

back down, just in case her enthusiasm might make Ms. Shelby decide to choose someone who knows how to raise their hand calmly. "Deja?" she says.

"A field trip to the aquarium," Deja declares, certain she is right.

Ms. Shelby smiles and shakes her head. That only starts a chorus of guesses from those who don't know how to raise their hands and wait to be recognized:

"A field trip to the zoo!"

"A field trip to Hamburger Hut!"

"A field trip to Waterworks Water Park!"

Ms. Shelby puts her finger to her lips and raises her other hand, looking around until everyone has done the same. When all is quiet she says, "We, I mean the whole school, will be having an election for student body president of Carver Elementary."

All mouths remain closed. Some frown a bit with disappointment. Nobody looks like they know what to say. While everyone is taking this in, Deja is making a decision. *That president is going to be me!* She smiles to herself as if she has already won.

"Of course, the election is only open to third-, fourth-, and fifth-graders. Mr. Brown wanted to keep it open only to the fourth and fifth grade, but I convinced him that we have some very capable third-graders at this school."

Deja sits up extra straight then, feeling that Ms. Shelby is talking about *her*. She looks around. Yolanda is sneaking sunflower seeds out of her book bag. ChiChi is coloring her nails with marker again. Ayanna is rearranging the items in her pencil box. Carlos is busy making something with torn bits of paper just inside his desk. A few bits of torn paper have drifted down on the floor around his chair. These do not seem like very capable third-graders to Deja.

Her eyes drift over to Antonia. Antonia is sitting ramrod straight, hands folded, with just a hint of a triumphant smile on her face. Deja frowns. Antonia looks as if she is just that capable person Ms. Shelby is talking about. Deja narrows her eyes. Then, as if Antonia can read her mind, she turns and looks directly at Deja and does a little eye roll.

Ms. Shelby continues talking about all the boring stuff. Deja looks as if she's listening, but she's really wondering why on earth they have to know all about elections. Ms. Shelby asks the class what qualities they think a student body president should have. Alyssa's hand flies up and

Deja knows that she probably doesn't have anything to say. Ms. Shelby calls on her and sure enough, she just lowers her eyes and smiles to herself, again.

Antonia raises her hand. "Antonia?" Ms. Shelby says.

"A good president should have a good home-work record," she says primly. Her hands are still folded.

"Definitely," Ms. Shelby says.

Deja quickly raises her hand, but Ms. Shelby calls on Carlos. "A good president should have straight A's."

That's just what Deja was going to say. Now she'll have to come up with something else. Ms. Shelby smiles kindly and says, "Well . . . they should at least be the kind of student who tries his or her best." Everyone knows that's just Ms. Shelby's polite way of saying, *"Wrong, Carlos. Dead wrong."* Deja's glad that she didn't get called on. She's surprised when she hears Ms. Shelby say, "Deja, you had your hand up."

Everyone turns to Deja, including Antonia, who has her eyebrows raised expectantly. Deja doesn't have anything to add—not yet. She hasn't had a chance to think. "A good president should be a . . ." Her voice trails off. She's going to be just like Alyssa. Always raising her hand with nothing to say. "A good president should be . . ." Deja can't help glancing at Antonia. Now Antonia has raised her eyebrows even more. "A good president should be someone who is . . ."

"Do you want me to come back to you?" Ms. Shelby offers.

Deja shakes her head. "A good student body president should be someone who is . . . *always fair!*" It comes to her all of a sudden, and she can tell by Ms. Shelby's smile that she has hit the jackpot.

"Excellent, Deja. We would want someone who is fair—no matter what. Someone who would think of everyone's benefit, not just a select few."

Deja doesn't even know what Ms. Shelby is talking about. She just knows that it sounds good and that her answer inspired all this extra talk. Nikki looks over at Deja and gives her the thumbs-up. Suddenly, Deja knows just what role Nikki is going to play in getting Deja elected as student body president of Carver Elementary School. Nikki will be her campaign manager.

"So . . . ," Ms. Shelby is moving on, having finished listing all the characteristics of a good student body president. Most of them were her own suggestions, since she had a hard time wringing appropriate answers from the class. It's after lunch recess and everyone is tired and wanting to hear *The Whipping Boy*. Ms. Shelby takes out the book, opens it to the right page, then half sits and half leans on her desk. However, she doesn't start reading right away. "Before I get back to our book, let me explain what comes next. Tomorrow before recess we'll have nominations. Each of you will get to nominate a classmate for the office of student body president. The student who gets the most nominations will represent our class and run in the upcoming school election."

Her words stir a little flutter of excitement in Deja's stomach. She looks around the room to see how many nominations she can count on. It's tricky. At least she knows she has Nikki's vote.

Ms. Shelby begins the story, but Deja's attention drifts from *The Whipping Boy* to the list on the whiteboard.

A good student body president is

 -*a student who has a good homework record.*

 -*a student who tries his/her best.*

 -*a student who is always fair.*

-a student who is always on time.

-a student who is enthusiastic.

-a student who works well with others.

-a student who listens to what others have to say.

-a student who is creative.

-a student who takes initiative.

-a student who is a problem solver.

Deja wonders about that list. Some of the characteristics are puzzling. For example, she doesn't quite know what the word *initiative* means. What is that, exactly? And how would someone be creative as student body president? She thinks she can work well with others, as long as they don't have a bunch of stupid ideas. She mostly tries her best, and she's almost always on time to school. She's mostly fair, even though Nikki sometimes says she isn't. She listens to others, she thinks, and she can solve problems—though she doesn't know what kind of problems would come up if she's president. But *initiative* . . . what on earth does *taking initiative* mean?

3

Let the Games Begin

"Who do you think is going to win the election?" Deja says as they skip down the school's front steps and turn toward their street. Deja asks this just to see if Nikki will say that it will be her, Deja.

"I don't know," Nikki says. "Maybe Gregory Johnson in fifth grade. He's real popular."

Deja is silent.

"Oh, no, wait," Nikki says. "Maybe Antonia. I betcha everyone's gonna vote for Antonia, because her mother brought cupcakes when our class's perfect attendance was in the newsletter."

Now Deja is annoyed. Why hasn't Nikki mentioned Deja?

"You know what?"

"What, Nikki?"

"It's probably not going to be Antonia. Everyone thinks she's stuck up. No, Antonia is not going to get it."

"Who are *you* going to nominate?" Deja asks, growing impatient.

"I don't know," Nikki says, frowning with concentration as if she's really giving it some thought. "Who are you going to nominate?"

"I'd have to nominate you, Nikki, since you're my best friend." Deja thinks this should be a big enough hint.

"But I don't want to run for student body president."

"But I'd still nominate you, since you're my best friend and all."

"But I just don't want to be student body president."

"I know you don't want to be student body president," Deja says, her voice a little raised. "But because you're my best friend, I'd nominate you."

"Please don't nominate me, Deja."

The conversation is not going in the direction that Deja wants. She decides to ask again. There is silence until finally Nikki says, "I guess I'm going to nominate you—unless you don't want to be student body president, either."

"No, I *want* to be president. I think I'd really be better than anyone else."

Nikki doesn't say anything, and Deja doesn't like that Nikki doesn't say anything. Finally Nikki says, "Okay, I'm nominating you, Deja."

"Thanks," Deja says simply. "And you can be my campaign manager, Nikki."

Deja has her mind on that extra candy Nikki is holding for her in her dresser drawer. After she gets home, as soon as she drops her backpack off and gets permission from Auntie Dee, she hurries over and knocks on Nikki's back door. Nikki opens it. She's eating a carrot stick.

"Guess what, Deja," Nikki says. "You get to eat dinner here tonight because your auntie has a meeting she has to go to."

That's even better, because now Deja can go over her campaign strategy with Nikki.

"Your auntie didn't tell you?" Nikki asks when Deja looks surprised.

"She was on the phone."

"Your auntie is always on the phone."

"No, she isn't," Deja says. "And when she is, it's because she does a lot of work at home. Lots of people work at home." Deja feels as if she has to defend Auntie Dee for some reason. "I want some of my candy," she adds.

When they go inside, Nikki's mom is sitting at the kitchen table folding clothes. Deja says hello politely, like Auntie always reminds her to do with grownups.

"Hi, Deja," Nikki's mom says. She sounds tired and sad. Deja has heard that same tone in Auntie's voice when she's tired. But then she remembers what Nikki said about her parents not speaking and the thought makes her uneasy. She follows Nikki up the stairs to her room.

"See?" Nikki says, collapsing on her bed and putting her chin in her hands. "See how my mom is acting? It doesn't look good."

"Maybe she's just tired."

"But she's never tired. She gets to stay home all day. Why would my mom be tired?"

"Nikki, just because parents aren't speaking doesn't mean they're going to get a divorce." Deja feels wise saying this to Nikki. She must have heard it somewhere. "Where's my candy?" she asks.

Nikki shrugs and points to her top dresser drawer. In the corner of the drawer is the white Candy Palace bag. Deja digs out a cherry sour whip. As she pops it in her mouth she wonders why she has to have the aunt that insists on healthy eating. What's wrong with a little candy every day? "Want some?" she asks, holding the bag out to Nikki.

Nikki barely looks up, but she still reaches out for the bag. Deja watches carefully as she rummages around and takes out three chocolate spiders, which Deja had wound up buying herself. Deja doesn't want her to take that many. But since Nikki looks so down, she doesn't say anything. They chew on their candy for a while. Finally, Deja says, "Who do you think will nominate me for student body president?"

"None of the boys, that's for sure."

"None of them?"

"Would you vote for one of the boys?"

Deja runs a few of the boys' names through her head. There is absolutely no boy that she can think of that she would nominate. Well, maybe Erik Castillo, since he's nice to everybody, follows directions, can sit still, and finishes his work in a timely manner.

As if Nikki is reading her mind, she says, "I'd nominate Erik, if I wasn't already going to nominate you."

"Which girls will nominate me?"

"Definitely not Antonia," Nikki says before reaching into Deja's white bag for another chocolate spider. Deja wonders why Nikki didn't just buy her own. They hear the front door close then and know that Nikki's dad is home. Nikki and Deja look at each other as if to say "Uh-oh . . ."

Deja can't tell that anything is different. Nikki's dad sits at the head of the table and Nikki's mom sits at the other end. Everyone is eating quietly and Deja is remembering to chew with her mouth closed. She looks down at her plate. Green beans (she doesn't really like green beans), baked fish (she'd rather it be fried), and wild rice. She doesn't like the hard black grains in the rice. The last time Deja ate at Nikki's, they had macaroni and cheese and fried chicken.

"What kind of fish is this?" Nikki's dad asks.

"Why?" Nikki's mom asks, and Nikki and Deja exchange wide-eyed looks. Nikki's mom doesn't sound happy and helpful. She sounds as if she is two moments away from being angry.

"Just wondering," Nikki's father says, and her mother doesn't even look up.

The rest of the meal is silent, and Deja can feel Nikki's unhappiness. But without meaning to, Deja's thoughts turn to who might nominate

her. It's way easier to think about the election than about Nikki's woes. Carefully, she begins to count on her fingers under the table. Rosario, ChiChi. . . . Wait. What if they nominate each other? Melinda. And Yolanda, since Deja gave her her banana pudding at lunch the week before. Deja doesn't like the taste of banana, but Yolanda didn't know that.

It's just at that moment that Deja realizes Nikki's mom is talking to her.

"Would you like more fish, Deja?"

She looks down at her plate. Fish is the only food she's eaten. There is still the mound of green beans waiting for her, and the wild rice with the black things. "No, thank you," she says. It's going to be hard enough getting through what is left.

After dinner, as soon as they flop down on Nikki's bed, Nikki bursts out, "See, see—what did I tell you? They're still not speaking."

"Gosh, Nikki, it'll blow over. You'll feel better if you put your mind on other things, like my campaign. Take out your pad. We need to list all the stuff we have to do."

Nikki takes her pad out of the special pouch

she wears around her neck, then sits with her pen poised, waiting for Deja to speak.

"We need to make campaign posters. We need to find out who everyone is nominating. We need to work on my speech . . ." Deja stops to think. Nikki rolls her eyes.

"We're going to have to poll everybody before school starts to see who they're nominating. So we have to get there early tomorrow."

"Poll people?" Nikki's voice sounds wary.

"Yeah, like when Auntie Dee and the block club wanted to find out if our neighbors wanted a stop sign at the corner of Fulton and Marin. They asked everyone on the block if they were in favor of it. Then they got a whole bunch of people to write letters to the city council and stuff. We'll just ask people who they're going to nominate. Then we count the ones who are planning to nominate me. Simple."

"You've got my nomination, so that's one," Nikki says.

"Two," Deja says. "I'm going to nominate myself." She nods her head once, quickly, and it makes her feel sure and confident.

4

The Lay of the Land

Deja stops Nikki at the schoolyard gate the next morning. The bell hasn't rung yet and from the yard entrance they can see the whole playground.

"Who's here?" Deja says.

"I see Yolanda." Nikki points across the yard to the line-up area. Already, Yolanda is calmly standing in Room Ten's line-up space all alone. She doesn't seem bothered. She just stares at the other children as they play.

"What's she doing?" Deja asks.

"She always lines up early," Nikki says. "Kids make fun of her when she tries to play. They say she runs funny. Because she's so fat."

"Let's go see who she's nominating," Deja says.

Yolanda's face takes on a cautious look as they approach. Nikki and Deja say hi, and Yolanda steps back a little and frowns, turning her head to the side but keeping her eyes locked first on Deja, then Nikki. "Hi," she says in a small voice.

"Who are you going to nominate?" Deja asks, diving in.

"Nominate?"

"For student body president of Carver Elementary."

"Oh, that," she says, and her mouth droops in disappointment. "I don't know yet."

"Are you nominating yourself?" Nikki asks.

"Why would I do that?"

"I'm nominating myself," Deja says confidently.

"You're not supposed to do that," Yolanda says with authority.

"Ms. Shelby didn't say we couldn't," Deja counters.

"Maybe she didn't think she had to," Yolanda says, making Deja wish she hadn't revealed this to Yolanda, who is all of a sudden taking on an annoying know-it-all manner. "Think of it. If everyone nominated themselves, there wouldn't be anyone to run. 'Cause *everyone* would have a nomination."

Deja ignores this and moves on to her point. "So who are you thinking about nominating—if you had to right now?"

Yolanda looks down and smiles as if she has something everyone wants and she—and only she—can choose to whom she will give it. After a few moments she says very decidedly, "Erik."

"A boy?" Nikki and Deja say together.

"He's nice. He never makes fun of people. He does his homework every day, he knows how to stay on task, he never talk—"

"Okay, you made your point," Deja interrupts. She's spotted ChiChi and Keisha across the yard and is ready to move on. She needs to get to them before the bell rings and it's time to line up. "Come on, Nikki."

"Bye, Yolanda," Nikki says as they turn toward ChiChi and Keisha, who are strolling around the perimeter of the yard like the fifth grade girls often do.

"Come on," Deja calls to Nikki over her shoulder.

"Hi, ChiChi and Keisha," she says in her friendliest tone. They stop and shield their eyes from the morning sun. "What are you guys doing?"

"Nothing. Just walking around," Keisha says.

"Yeah, we're just walking around," ChiChi

agrees. They look as if they're being interrupted—as if they might have been talking about someone. Maybe about the person they're going to nominate for president. For a moment the four of them stand there, saying nothing. Deja breaks the silence first.

"So who are you two nominating?"

"Nominating?" Keisha asks.

ChiChi looks down and to the side.

"For student body president of Carver Elementary," Deja says, expecting them to say they're nominating each other.

"Oh, that. I think I'm going to nominate Casey," ChiChi says.

"Casey?"

"Yeah, she seems nice."

"You're not supposed to vote for someone 'cause they're nice," Deja says. "You're supposed to vote for the person you think can do the job."

"But I think Casey can do the job."

Deja is at a loss for a moment. Just as she opens her mouth to ask ChiChi why she thinks that Casey can do the job, the freeze bell rings. She's left with her mouth hanging open for a moment, until she remembers that you don't have to freeze your mouth. The second bell rings and she and Nikki walk to the line. Deja tries to take her place in front of Ralph, but he moves forward as if to squeeze her out. "Back up, Ralph," she warns him. Ralph looks at Ms. Shelby walking briskly toward the class and steps back. Deja takes her place and the students march across the schoolyard toward their class-room.

Soon everyone is in their seats, fishing through desks for their morning journals and checking the board for the topic of the day. Deja quickly retrieves her journal from the mess in her desk, opens it up, writes the date at the top of the page, then checks the board for the topic.

Her shoulders slump. *The Person I Most Admire.* Every once in a while, Ms. Shelby pulls that one out of her collection of topics. And every time, Deja is at a loss. She looks over at Nikki, already knowing that Nikki's pencil will be skittering across the page with so much to write she can hardly get it all down. She checks Antonia. Antonia is staring off into space, but then she calmly picks up her pencil and begins to write. Deja thinks and thinks. She can't write about Martin Luther King, Jr. She's done that already. She can't write about Ms. Shelby. She tried that a few months ago and found herself challenged to fill up a page.

Then, suddenly, it occurs to her. She has never written about Auntie Dee! She quickly begins, and it's hard to write as fast as the thoughts spilling over each other in her head.

My Auntie Dee is the best person. She takes care of me even tho she doesn't have to because she is not my mother or my father she does it just because she loves me. I love my Auntie Dee. My mother passed away when I was real little and my father can't take care of me. So my Auntie Dee takes care of me. I have my own room and it even has a desk in it because Auntie Dee says everyone has to have a place to settle down and get to work and I have a bookshelf too because Auntie Dee says one of the most important thing a person can do is love to read and, she cooks good too but she cooks a lot of healthy stuff so I have to eat lots of vegetables and cookies made with apple juice that don't taste all that good. And one time she made a cake that didn't have any eggs or butter. It tasted really good. But I had a real cake for my birthday with lavender icing and light pink flowers made from real sugar. And it tasted good too.

Deja stops and looks at what she's written. Ms. Shelby always has to remind everyone how important it is to read over what they've written when they finish, because then they'll see all the skipped words and misspelled words and run-on sentences. There it is: a run-on sentence in the middle of her great paragraph, which takes up a full page because she wrote kind of big. It's a long one. Just when she's trying to figure out where to put the periods and capitalizations, she hears the timer—the one in the shape of an egg—go off. Time's up. Deja sighs, looking at the page, and

hopes Ms. Shelby is not going to ask for the journals to be turned in today so she can do a spot check. Once a week Ms. Shelby looks over journal entries and writes comments at the top of the page.

Happily, she doesn't direct the class to turn in their journals. She just moves to the front of the room and looks around as if she is readying herself to make an important announcement. Deja puts her journal away and sits with her hands folded, waiting for Ms. Shelby to get the class's attention.

While she waits, she glances around, attempting to determine which kids might nominate her. She looks over at Erik. He has already pulled his reading workbook out of his desk and is waiting calmly for their teacher to tell them the page number.

She checks Casey. Casey's nose is buried in her Sustained Silent Reading book. She's doing just what Ms. Shelby says to do when you find that you're an early bird. Ms. Shelby has to tell the goof-offs over and over, "It's not your job to disturb your classmates when you finish a task early. You can always take out your SSR book. I should never see anyone doing absolutely nothing." Deja doesn't know why Ms. Shelby bothers to repeat this. The same kids have to be reminded again and again.

Deja digs around in her desk for her Sustained Silent Reading book. It's way in the back and the cover has gotten dog-eared from having been squished amidst the mess. She smoothes the cover, then opens it up, not knowing exactly where she left off. She stares at the page, not actually reading, but trying very hard to give the impression that she is.

"So, class . . ." Ms. Shelby says in a very serious tone. *Here it comes,* Deja thinks. *Finally we get to the important stuff.*

"We need to go over something before we move on to reading activities." Deja folds her hands and smiles. She feels excitement and a little fear ripple through her. She's waiting to hear the word *nominations.* It's coming. Casey slips a bookmark into her book, closes it, and puts it away. Erik gazes at the workbook on his desk and then looks at Ms. Shelby. Deja sits up straight.

"I have an announcement, so pay attention. We are going to trade play areas with Mr. Beaumont's class. They want to finish their sockball tournament from last week, so we're going to have their tetherball/foursquare area for the next couple of days."

A few boys groan. Deja groans too, inwardly, because this is not what she was expecting. In fact, Ms. Shelby is acting as if she's forgotten all about the election, even though she'd made such a big deal about it and gotten the class all excited. Deja's hand flies up before she knows it.

"Yes, Deja," Ms. Shelby says in a distracted tone of voice.

"What about nominations?"

"Oh, yes. Sure. That's on our agenda."

Deja checks the agenda posted next to the whiteboard. There it is: *1:30–1:45 Nominations.*

Actually, this works out better. It means she still has morning and lunch recess to convince everyone to nominate her.

5

Nominations

Morning recess can't come fast enough. But when it does, Deja takes her time exiting the classroom. She holds Nikki back as well. As soon as they reach the schoolyard, Deja grabs Nikki's arm. "This is what I want you to do, Nikki," she begins.

Nikki's already eyeing the line for tetherball. She looks at Deja suspiciously. "What?" she says.

"I want you to go around and find out who everyone's nominating. Just make a tally mark on your writing pad for everybody who's voting for me." As Deja is saying this, she notes Nikki's brows sinking lower and lower. Her mouth turns down in a frown.

"I don't want to do that, Deja. I want to play tetherball."

"Come on, Nikki. You're my campaign manager. That's what they do. They take polls."

Nikki sighs and drags herself off, holding her pad and pen. Deja looks after her for a while before finding a bench to sit on and wait for the results. She can't help watching as Nikki makes the rounds. Most of the kids in the class look either surprised to have their play interrupted, or annoyed. Finally, Nikki comes back. She's walking briskly and her mouth looks as if she is holding back a smile.

"Okay, tell me how many are nominating me," Deja says.

Nikki sits down beside her and flips open her pad. Deja immediately sees seven tally marks.

"I told everybody that you wanted to be nominated so you got Keisha, Anna, Rosario, Melinda, me, Yolanda—I got her to change her mind—and Erik."

"Erik?"

"He said he's not the president type and that's what I told Yolanda, so she's going to nominate you."

Deja thinks about this. *Only seven?* "What

about Ayanna?" Deja had seen Nikki talking to Ayanna for a long time.

"Oh, she's nominating Antonia."

Deja scans the yard. When she spots Ayanna, she watches her for a few moments, trying to figure out why she has decided to nominate Antonia. Deja's never even seen them playing together. What was that about? "Did you ask everybody?"

"I couldn't find everybody. Some kids might have been in the bathroom."

"Hmm." Deja needs to think about this.

The freeze bell rings and she sits very still, thinking about the number *seven*.

Lunch recess doesn't go as planned, either. When Nikki comes back with her pen and pad to join Deja on the bench next to the second grade portable, she has nothing much to report.

"Well," she announces cheerfully, "I told almost everyone that you want to be nominated, so maybe they'll nominate you."

Deja looks at Nikki, but her mind is on the number seven. *Seven.*

After a chapter of *The Whipping Boy*, which Deja listens to with her head on the desk and her eyes closed, Ms. Shelby says, "Okay, let's move on to the nominations. Let me go over some rules first. You will be getting a ballot. How many know what a ballot is?"

Oh, boy, Deja thinks. *Now we have to go through everyone trying to explain what a ballot is. Why can't Ms. Shelby just tell us?* Ms. Shelby moves to the whiteboard and picks up one of the dry-erase markers. She holds it up, waiting for hands.

Carlos waves his around with a look of certainty on his face. "It's a piece of paper and has a bunch of people's names on it and they put a check next to the person's name who they want."

Ms. Shelby looks out the window for a moment and Deja knows she's trying to think of a way to reword it so that it will be close to the answer she has in mind.

"Well, yes. That's basically what it is." She returns the marker to the tray in front of the whiteboard.

Deja's relieved. Ms. Shelby has decided to just tell them. "I am going to give each of you a ballot. On it you will find the names of your classmates as well as your own. You are to put your name at the top, then put a check beside the name of the person you think will make the best student body president of Carver Elementary School."

She stops to look around the room. "Now, I want to make it very clear that you are not—*not*—to select yourself." She stops and glances around the room again as if she's addressing this only to certain students, not the entire class. "Your name will be on the ballot so it will be easy to see if you chose yourself."

With that she picks up the stack of ballots and passes them out a batch at a time to the person sitting at the front of each row. Now Deja feels an agitation in the pit of her stomach. It's going to take extra time because there's always a knucklehead who can't just take the paper on top and simply pass the remainder behind them.

Sure enough, Alyssa is Miss Butterfingers when the ballots get passed back to her. Ralph drops them over his shoulder, probably thinking Alyssa's hand is ready to receive them. But she's busy daydreaming, so they spill onto the floor. Then it takes a few more seconds for her to look at them helplessly as if she doesn't know what to do.

Deja leaps out of her seat to scoop up the papers and pass them out to everyone in her row who doesn't have one. "Thank you, Deja," Ms. Shelby says.

When everyone has a ballot and has written his or her name at the top—and several students have to be reminded to do this—Ms. Shelby instructs them to mark their votes.

Deja hesitates, pencil poised. She'd assumed she'd nominate herself. But Ms. Shelby said that wasn't allowed and now she has to come up with someone else to vote for. Not Nikki, because she doesn't want to be student body president. Not any of the boys, of course. Melinda? Keisha? Rosario? ChiChi? Yolanda?

It occurs to her then. Yolanda is perfect! Deja will probably be the only one voting for Yolanda. That way, she won't be giving her vote to someone who might be nominated. Deja puts a big fat check next to Yolanda's name. Perfect.

At last the ballots are collected and Antonia, who happens to be general helper that week, gets to go up to the whiteboard to help Ms. Shelby tally the vote. Ms. Shelby has put everyone's names on the board.

Deja thinks Carlos should be up there reading off the ballots, since Ms. Shelby took over his paper monitor job when she passed out the ballots. Instead Antonia stands there, looking important and smiling secretively as if she already knows who's gotten the nomination.

"Let's begin," Ms. Shelby says cheerfully.

In a quiet voice—too quiet, Deja thinks—Antonia begins to report the nominations. "Richard," Antonia says, then places the ballot on Ms. Shelby's desk. Ms. Shelby carefully places a tally mark beside his name.

Deja bites her lip.

"Here's one for Erik," Antonia says.

Deja's sure boys nominated Richard and Erik. She feels her heart pounding in her chest.

"Deja," Antonia continues, her face revealing no emotion.

Deja feels some relief.

"Yolanda," Antonia says.

That must be her ballot, Deja thinks, but then Antonia says Yolanda's name again. Now there are two checks beside Yolanda's name. She is officially winning.

Antonia calls out her own name, then Erik's, then Richard's again, then her own.

Where's Nikki's ballot and those of the five other people who'd said they'd choose Deja?

"Deja," Antonia says dryly.

Deja watches while Ms. Shelby puts a check beside her name. *Now that's more like it,* she thinks.

"Yolanda," Antonia says next.

Once again, Yolanda is ahead.

Who are all these people nominating Yolanda? Deja wonders.

"Erik," Antonia says. Now Richard, Antonia, and Deja are tied for second place, with Yolanda and Erik tied for first. Deja quickly takes a head count. She's certain the boys are nominating boys. There are nine boys in the class and eleven girls. That means so far only five boys and seven girls have had their ballots read. The boys have four more nominations and the girls have four more. What if some of the girls chose Erik or Richard? Deja's heart sinks. Then Antonia says Deja's name two times in a row. The second announcement comes after a long pause, to the point that Ms. Shelby offers to look at the ballot. Perhaps the check beside a name was too light.

But no. Deja hears her name spoken softly but clearly. "Deja."

She looks down and smiles. She's leading.

"Keisha," Antonia says. Then, "ChiChi."

They nominated each other, Deja is certain. She tallies the marks. Unfortunately, the girls are finished, but the boys still have their four votes left. *It's over,* she thinks.

"Yolanda," Antonia announces, with a hint of

triumph in her voice. Yolanda has caught up to Deja. And it was probably with a boy nomination.

"Erik," Antonia says.

"Yolanda," she continues. This time she looks at Deja and smirks. Yolanda has taken the lead again.

It could be a lost cause, Deja thinks. One more to go, and she and Erik are the only two who can benefit. The others don't have enough votes. She waits to hear what Antonia has to say, but Antonia is silent. Everyone looks at her, waiting. Ms. Shelby, with the marker poised to make the next tally mark, looks over her shoulder.

"I can't make this out," Antonia finally says. "It looks like this person voted for two people."

"Let me see that," Ms. Shelby says.

Antonia holds up the ballot for Ms. Shelby to check.

"You're right. It seems as if this person selected two people. One tally mark looks erased, but not completely. I can't be sure who this person intended to nominate. Erik, could you help us out and tell me whom you meant to nominate?" She takes the ballot out of Antonia's hand and brings it to Erik to verify his nomination. Erik studies the ballot for what seems like a long time.

"I nominated Deja," he says.

At first Deja can't believe it. With just three words spoken, she has tied with Yolanda. Yolanda! She might as well have the nomination. Yolanda is definitely not going to be a problem. Ms. Shelby's voice interrupts her thoughts.

"Looks like we'll need to have a runoff between Deja and Yolanda," Ms. Shelby says. "But not today. We've already used up too much math time. We'll continue with the nominations tomorrow."

6

Runoff Election

Deja is lying on her bed, tossing a balled sock into the air. Maybe she should go out and practice her Ping-Pong serve. It's still light outside. She looks out the window at the Ping-Pong table in the driveway. No, that wouldn't be fun. She can hear Auntie Dee downstairs in the kitchen making tofu burgers and sweet potato french fries—but they're not going to be fried. They're going to be baked. They're going to be fake fries. And all through dinner, Auntie Dee is going to keep saying, "Aren't these yummy? Aren't these just like real french fries?" And Deja is going to think that they're not at all like real french fries, and why can't they have real fries at least some of the time?

Still, Deja is a little bit hungry. But mainly she is thinking about who everyone nominated. After all, she was supposed to get seven nominations, not five. If she had gotten the seven, she'd have easily been the nominee. Deja likes the word *nominee*. She *will* be the nominee. The phone rings but she doesn't make a move to get it, since it is probably for Auntie Dee. Then she hears her name being called. *It's probably Nikki,* she thinks as she goes down the stairs.

It *is* Nikki, and her voice is full of excitement. "Deja, guess what!"

In the second before Nikki speaks, Deja imagines that Nikki has spent the time since she got home from school making phone calls to all of their classmates, and they have all told her that they are choosing Deja. They had just nominated Yolanda to make her feel better about being fat. But that is not what Nikki has to say.

"My father told a joke at dinner and my mom laughed. They're talking again!" Deja is disappointed. Not for Nikki—she's happy for Nikki. But she's disappointed for herself. She had hoped Nikki was calling with new information about the election.

"Great, Nikki," Deja says. "How many votes do you think I'm going to get tomorrow?"

"I don't know," Nikki says—and rather impatiently, Deja thinks. She knows Nikki's mind is not really on the runoff. It's still on her mom and dad. "Look at how many people picked Yolanda. I gotta go. See you tomorrow."

When she hangs up, Deja is still thinking about the election. Five people nominated Yolanda today. Who were those kids? She thinks about it while she watches TV later with Auntie Dee. She thinks about it while she brushes her teeth, while she lays out her clothes for the next day (which Auntie always insists she do), and while she makes her lunch and puts it away in the refrigerator. Which kids were the kids who chose Yolanda?

On her way to school the next morning, Deja can hardly follow Nikki's constant chatter about how her daddy made her mom breakfast, how her daddy is taking her mom out for dinner, how her mom is going to call Auntie Dee to see if she can babysit tonight, and won't that be great because they can plan election strategy together.

Deja's ears perk up at the mention of election strategy. That's right—when she gets the nomination, she's going to have to immediately come up with a *strategy*. She tugs on Nikki's sleeve. "Listen,

Nikki, as soon as everyone's in line—before Ms. Shelby gets there—I'm going to find out who nominated Yolanda." Nikki doesn't say anything, but Deja thinks she hears a little sigh.

As soon as the bell rings, releasing everyone from their freeze positions, the Room Ten students mosey over to their line. A few are yawning, a few are staring off into space. Everyone looks as if they're not quite ready to start the day. Deja has to be quick and direct. She looks toward the school building, then at Mr. Brown, the principal, who is busy with a parent. Happily, he's facing the other way.

Deja starts at the back and moves forward. She has to be careful. Once everyone is lined up, no one is allowed to talk or get out of line. Some kids blink at her uncomprehendingly before they understand what she's asking. Some get a bit hostile, thinking she's going to get mad at them for not nominating her. Only three admit to voting for Yolanda. She skips over Antonia, knowing Antonia wouldn't tell her one way or the other. But Deja suspects Antonia voted for Yolanda, too, thinking, like Deja, that her vote wouldn't make a difference because it would be the only one. Deja scoots back to her place in line just as she sees Ms. Shelby making her way across the yard. She's feeling pretty confident. She's going to get that nomination. She just knows it. As they begin walking toward the school doors, it occurs to Deja that she didn't see Yolanda.

When Deja enters the classroom, her eyes immediately go to the posted agenda. She scans down for the magic words. Today Ms. Shelby has termed it *Election Activity*. It's scheduled right after morning recess. Deja checks the morning journal subject and her heart lifts. *Open Topic.* When Ms. Shelby can't think of a topic, she lets them write what they want. Sometimes she'll pick someone from each table to share what they've written. Deja hopes it's one of those times. She dives right in.

Why I Think I Would make the best President Carver Elementary School Ever Had!

I think I would make the best president Carver Elementary School ever had because I would be the best president Carver Elementary School ever had.

She reads that over. It doesn't sound right, but she presses on. She needs to finish.

I really care about my school. I care about what people think of it. If it is bad with a lot of bad kids no one will want to come here. If there are a lot of fights and people writing all over the walls. People will think it's a bad school. But it's not a bad school. My school is good. And I will make it better. I will make it so that a lot of kids will want to come here and there parents will want them to come here too.

Deja's proud of herself for spelling "too," t-o-o. She's proud that she remembered to indent. Ms. Shelby hates when they don't indent. Ms. Shelby says, "I have to tell the same people over and over to indent. Why is that?" Deja is happy that she is not one of those people.

I want lots of new kids to come to our school. We have had the same ol kids for a long time. I would make it so new kids came to Carver Elementary School. Smart kids. I would make it so we have better food in the cafeteria. I would make it so the bad kids had detension for five hours after school so they wouldn't fight anymore and make our school look bad. I would do a good job for our school so it would become famous all over the country.

Deja hears Ms. Shelby's timer. She stops writing and begins to read what she has written. It sounds pretty good. Her hand flies up before Ms. Shelby can direct them to put away their journals and take out their workbooks.

Ms. Shelby looks up from the attendance roster. "Yes, Deja," she says, sounding like her mind is still on attendance.

"Can I read mine?"

"Read yours? Oh, sure. In a nice, loud voice."

Ms. Shelby doesn't really have to tell Deja to read in a loud voice. She never mutters or holds her paper in front of her face, blocking the sound waves like some people. While Deja reads, she notices Ms. Shelby taking attendance and making notations in her class book, the one that has everyone's scores and attendance and homework. The scary book.

When Deja finishes, she looks around. Some kids were paying attention but some were doing other things. Deja thinks Ms. Shelby should have made everyone give her their undivided attention—that she should have instructed Deja to wait until everyone was listening. But Ms. Shelby wasn't even listening herself. Not really.

"Good, Deja," she says. "You may sit down now."

Deja sits down and looks around. Did anyone even hear what she had to say? Ayanna is drawing daisies with a purple marker on her journal cover. Carlos has some kind of doughy substance he's pulled out of his desk. He's keeping it out of sight as much as possible as he rolls it into a long snake. He's completely engrossed. And Ralph . . . Ralph is playing with the flat marbles from the classroom's mancala game! No wonder they always have to ask Ms. Shelby for more pieces from the stash in her desk drawer. Ralph's been taking them home! Deja feels a flash of anger. She's about to raise her hand again when Ms. Shelby tells them to put everything away and take out their workbooks.

"Yolanda is not even at school," Deja says to Nikki on the way to the tetherball court. "It's like she doesn't even care if she's nominated or not. I think it's because she knows she can't win."

"What makes you think she can't win the nomination?" Nikki asks.

"The kids who chose Yolanda are the ones who wanted to be nominated themselves," Deja explains as they approach the line of kids waiting to play tetherball. "So they didn't give their vote to someone who might be getting a bunch of other nominations. They thought that their nomination for Yolanda would be her only one. And so it was kind of safe. Get it?"

"Wow," Nikki says, but Deja wonders if she really followed her logic.

ChiChi gets out, and the line advances. Deja grows excited. She's good at tetherball. Ms. Shelby instituted all these hard rules like no holding the ball. You have to keep it going. And no slinging the ball by the rope. You have to keep it going by punching it with your fist or smacking it with your open hand. Ayanna is out, and then Rosario. At last it is Deja's turn. She's up against Keisha. Keisha's just as good as Deja. It's her serve. She hits it high so that it sails over Deja's head. She jumps to smack the ball back, but it's out of reach. It's winding high around the pole and Keisha is keeping it going. Finally, Deja jumps and smacks it hard to send it going the other way, unwinding from the pole. She punches it again, thinking she's got the upper hand. But Keisha is ready. She hits it back with both hands balled into a single fist. It's coming too fast and high for Deja to get at. It's moving so quickly around the pole that Deja is not able to send it the other way. Before she knows it, the ball has completely wound around the pole and she is out.

Deja moves to the back of the line, a little stunned. She had been sure she was going to win.

"Okay," Ms. Shelby says as soon as they've taken their seats and have settled down. "It is after recess and, as promised, we are about to have our runoff. It's a shame Yolanda isn't here, but she's home sick. Her mother called the office before school. So she's going to miss the excitement." The whole time Ms. Shelby is talking, she is passing out a slender ballot with just Deja's and Yolanda's names on it. Today she's not doing the "take one and pass it back" routine, which can cause so much confusion. She seems to be in a rush to get class elections over with so they can move on to more important matters.

Deja suddenly has butterflies in her stomach. Ms. Shelby skips over her as she passes out the ballots. She explains that since this is a runoff

between just Yolanda and Deja, they won't be voting. "Well, Yolanda won't be voting anyway, since she's not here," Ms. Shelby mutters, almost to herself. "So everyone, mark your ballots quickly, then fold them in half and hold them up."

Everyone does just as she says. They mark their ballots then hold them up so Ms. Shelby can come around and pluck them out of their hands. She quickly writes Deja's and Yolanda's names on the board. It seems she's going to do everything herself. Deja thinks she must be in a hurry.

When all the tally marks are placed beside each name, Deja has gotten sixteen votes to Yolanda's four. Deja knows two people voted for Yolanda: Antonia and her best friend, Casey. But who were the others?

Who cares? Deja thinks. She is now the official nominee of Ms. Shelby's third grade class. Hah, hah, and *hah!*

"So there's a meeting for all us candidates during afternoon recess tomorrow," Deja says to Nikki.

"Mmm-hmm," Nikki says. It is bedtime and they're sharing Deja's bed for the night. Deja is on the window side. She always sleeps on the window side of the bed. Auntie said Nikki might as well spend the night, since her parents are going to be late getting back from dinner.

"They're getting along really good now," Nikki says. "I'm so glad." She yawns.

"I told you. You were worried for nothing," Deja says. She really wants to get back to the election and her candidacy. "So at the meeting we're going to get all the rules for the election. Plus we have to give a speech on Tuesday in front of the whole school about why we'd be the best and stuff." Deja pauses for Nikki's response.

"Mmm-hmm," Nikki says.

"I'm going to ask Auntie Dee if I can get a new outfit for my speech. I want something lavender because it's my favorite color. What do you think, Nikki?"

Silence.

"Nikki?"

Silence. Nikki has fallen asleep.

7

The New and
Improved Deja

Deja has a new sense of herself now that she is running for president of the entire school. *Her* entire school. As she and Nikki approach Carver Elementary, she actually feels a new kind of . . . *pride.* Yes, she has to call it pride—for the old brown brick building and broad cement steps. For the grass, even the dying patches, and the big sycamore tree with its huge exposed roots that look like boa constrictors hiding in the dirt. She feels important. *Important.* That's the word. The whole day she feels this way.

When Ms. Shelby reprimands certain students for waiting until after recess to raise their hands for permission to get water or go to the restroom, Deja feels as if she's on Ms. Shelby's side. She, too, can't understand why they continue to do this when they know better. She feels as put out as Ms. Shelby must. Being a candidate for student body president of Carver Elementary School has changed her. She now looks at her classmates as . . . well, more babyish than she.

During lunchtime, as she sits gazing down the table at the kids of Room Ten, she can really see this. First of all, ChiChi, who is lunch monitor this week, isn't even recording in her special notebook that Ralph Buyer is, at that very moment, sticking his drinking straw up his nose and turning his head from side to side for all to see. No, ChiChi is busy talking to Keisha. In fact, they're exchanging Cherry Berries and Lemon Berries with each other under the table. What kind of lunch monitor is that? And Nikki, her own best friend, is laughing at something Ayanna has said while she's still eating. Everyone knows that's dangerous. That should definitely be reported so Ms. Shelby can remind them that people can choke that way. The whole lunch scene is disgusting to Deja.

It's so disgusting that as soon as students enter the classroom and settle into their seats to prepare for the next installment of *The Whipping Boy,* Deja raises her hand. Ms. Shelby doesn't notice. She just moves to the "How Am I Doing?" chart and says, "ChiChi, do you have anything to report to me?"

ChiChi looks caught off-guard. She makes a show of considering Ms. Shelby's question by taking out the lunch book and flipping through the pages.

Deja puts her hand down but sits forward in her chair and looks back and forth between Ms. Shelby and ChiChi. She needs to say something. Before she has even decided what to say, her hand flies up again.

Ms. Shelby turns to Deja. "Yes, Deja."

"Ms. Shelby, ChiChi is not a good lunch monitor. She wasn't even looking or writing anything down in the tablet when a whole bunch of kids were not showing good lunch table behavior. Ralph was putting straws up his nose—"

"It was one straw!" Ralph interrupts.

The class bursts into laughter and Deja looks around, frowning.

"Class, please. Go on, Deja," Ms. Shelby says with a sigh. She always does a lot of sighing in the afternoon.

Now the whole class has turned toward Deja. They seem to be filled with anticipation. A few have half smiles on their faces.

Deja begins again. "Okay . . . Ralph put *a* straw up his nose. Keisha *and* ChiChi were eating Cherry Berries . . ."

"I was not eating Cherry Berries!" Keisha protests. "I had Lemon Berries and we weren't either eating them. We were just trading for *after school.* We weren't either gonna eat them. We were just trading!"

Ms. Shelby holds up her hand. "What are the rules about candy at school, Keisha?"

Keisha looks down. "No candy at school," she says in a quiet voice.

"That's right." Ms. Shelby changes Keisha's, ChiChi's, and Ralph's behavior cards from green to orange, the warning color. "ChiChi, if I get a report like this tomorrow, I'm going to have to get a new lunch monitor. Is that clear?"

ChiChi looks down. "Yeah."

"Pardon me?" Ms. Shelby says.

"Yes, Ms. Shelby."

"Thank you, Deja." Ms. Shelby picks up *The Whipping Boy* and opens it to where she left off the day before.

Deja waves her hand. "But I'm not finished, Ms. Shelby."

The whole class turns to Deja once again.

"Yes, Deja?"

"Nikki was doing something that was very, very dangerous. That *you* always tell us is very, very dangerous," Deja says, explaining herself, for now Nikki is staring at her. It gives Deja pause, but she continues. "Nikki was laughing really hard while she was eating. And you always told us that a person could choke if they do that."

When Deja finishes, she's surprised that Ms. Shelby doesn't say anything right away. It puts Deja in a funny spot. She can feel Nikki's displeasure and she isn't getting immediate approval from Ms. Shelby. Now she sits, waiting for Ms. Shelby to praise her for being the only one who noticed this hazardous activity, thereby preventing a big disaster in the future.

Finally Ms. Shelby turns to Deja and says, "Thank you again, Deja. Class, please remember that when you are eating you should refrain from laughing. You could choke." Then she picks up the book and begins to read.

Deja can't really concentrate on *The Whipping Boy*, though. She doesn't like the tone she heard in Ms. Shelby's voice. It sounded bland, not mad enough. She should have made what Deja told her more important. Deja's thoughts turn to Nikki. She wonders what she is thinking. Right then it seems like she can actually feel Nikki's thoughts. They seem to be hanging over the classroom like a big sour cloud. At one point, she chances a quick look over at Nikki. She is sitting with her chin in her hand, looking down at her desk. Is she frowning a little bit? Deja thinks that she is.

The same sour cloud seems to be following them after school as they walk home. Nikki is quiet, and Deja is chatty. First, she talks about the speech she has to give on Tuesday, five days away. Then she talks about what she will wear. When she notices that Nikki isn't commenting, she says, "What do you think I should wear, Nikki?"

Nikki takes a moment and then she says, "Wear what you want."

Deja looks over at her. "Why are you sounding like that?"

"Like what?" Nikki asks.

"All mad and stuff."

Nikki shrugs. "I'm not mad."

"Then how come you're acting mad?"

"I'm not acting mad. You asked me what you should wear and I said wear what you want."

Deja thinks about this for a bit. She opens her mouth to say something, but she can't think of anything to counter Nikki's logic. They walk the rest of the way home in silence. When they get to

Nikki's house, Deja says, "You want to play some Ping-Pong?"

"Nah, I don't think so," Nikki says. "See you later, Deja." She turns up her walkway.

Deja feels a little bit at a loss. She was going to tell Nikki it was time to work on the campaign posters, but somehow she knows Nikki will enjoy refusing to help her. Auntie has already bought poster boards and everything. Deja guesses she'll have to do them on her own. Well, who needs Nikki, anyway? She can come up with the slogans herself. She nods her head confidently, but she wishes she felt more certain about it.

The next morning, bright and early—even earlier than usual—Deja knocks on Nikki's back door. "Oh, Deja," Nikki's mother says when she opens it. She's still in her pajamas and robe and she has a coffeepot in her hand. Suddenly, Deja feels silly standing there with her posters. At least they're in a large bag so that no one can easily see the not-so-good job she did on them.

Auntie Dee always says that Deja needs to develop more patience. But because she had to work on her campaign posters all by herself, she got a little bit hurried. She misspelled too many words on one, according to Auntie Dee, so instead of having three posters to hang up around the school, she only has two. She'll put one on the wall just outside Room Ten, and one by the front office. She had wanted to post one on the fence beside the schoolyard gate, but that's not to be.

"What do you have there?" Nikki's mom asks.

"My campaign posters."

"Oh, for the school election. How exciting." She smiles down at Deja; a smile that seems full of encouragement. "Who else is running?"

"There's this boy named Arthur from Mr. Beaumont's third grade; a girl named Sheena from Mrs. Miller's third grade; me; two kids from the two fourth grades, Lashonda and . . . I forgot the other one's name; this girl named Paula from fifth grade; and Gregory Johnson from the fifth grade." She says his whole name because everyone always says his whole name.

"Wow, so you have some real competition. Let me see your posters."

Nikki's mom moves the salt and pepper shakers and a napkin holder that looks like an apple cut in half to make room for Deja's posters. Deja stands there. She realizes that she doesn't want to put her mistakes and poor quality posters on display, but she knows she can't get out of it.

She takes her time pulling out the first poster. VOTE 4 DEJA SHE'S THE 1! Deja looks at it as if she's seeing it for the first time. It has a big apple tree. Why did she put an apple tree on it? Probably because she knows how to draw a tree with apples kind of good.

"Oh," Nikki's mom says. "Okay, well . . . that's certainly some poster."

Deja looks at the lettering. She had tried to make bubble letters but she never really learned how. She likes the balloons that she drew floating above the tree and colored with blue and red markers. She put a little square on each to make them look bright and shining. The squares turned out looking a tiny bit like doors, but maybe people wouldn't look at them like that. Then she had tried to decorate the misshapen bubble letters with glitter and there were some globs that got in the wrong places, but maybe people wouldn't notice that, either.

Just as she's pulling out the second poster, which actually looks a little bit worse than the first, Nikki shows up. There they stand, the three of them, looking down on a green poster with many, many noticeable eraser marks. The marks make it look stripped of color in too many places. Deja kept misspelling *serious*.

First, she spelled it *cirreus*. When it didn't look right, she took it to Auntie Dee. Auntie told her the correct spelling. But Deja still accidentally left in the extra *r*. Even after she made the corrections, FOR A GOOD SERIOUS PRESIDENT, VOTE FOR DEJA! YES DEJA! looked too small and it wasn't centered.

Standing next to her, Deja can feel Nikki's regret that she had left her on her own.

"I had another poster but I kind of messed it up. So, I just have these two."

"I see," Nikki's mom said. "Did your aunt see these?"

"She was real busy, so I just did them by myself."

"I see," Nikki's mom said again. Then she smiled another encouraging smile.

The campaign posters, with Post-its on them designating where they are to be hung, have to be turned into the office. Deja's relieved that hers are still in the big bag. She gives it to Mrs. Marker, the office lady. But the bag doesn't help when Room Ten is dismissed for recess and everyone sees the poster beside the door. The laughter begins then, and seems to follow her around the yard all during recess.

"Deja, what happened to your posters?" Carlos yells as he runs by.

"Deja, who did your poster? Your baby brother?" Richard adds.

"I don't even have a brother," Deja calls back. Then she turns to see Ayanna, ChiChi, and Keisha with their heads together, laughing and whispering as they wait for their turns at tetherball. When Deja gets in line behind them, they suddenly stop. Then ChiChi starts to giggle again and Keisha and Ayanna soon join in. Deja knows they're laughing at her.

Antonia announces calmly, "Lashonda has the best posters."

"No," Ralph counters. "Gregory Johnson's posters are better. They look more *professional*." Deja wishes everybody would just stop talking about the posters. Ralph probably doesn't even really know what the word *professional* means. She can't wait until recess is over.

Ralph gets into the tetherball court just as the freeze bell rings. He doesn't get to do his killer serve. Hah, hah, and *hah!*

8

Campaign Speeches and Campaign Promises

"Listen to this, Nikki," Deja says on Sunday afternoon. Nikki sits on her porch working on a lanyard key chain for her father. Deja stands on the walkway before her with her speech in her hand. At ten o'clock Tuesday morning, Deja is going to have to get up onstage in the auditorium in front of the whole school and tell why she, a third-grader, would be the best student body president of Carver Elementary School. She wonders if any of the fourth- or fifth-graders will laugh at her.

Deja walks back and forth with her index cards. Nikki looks up from the lanyard key chain. She plans to make a matching one for her mom. "I'm listening," Nikki says.

Deja clears her throat. "Now really listen, because I'm going to ask you questions afterward."

"I'm listening."

Deja has already read her speech to Auntie Dee, who helped her with the opening and made a few suggestions so her message would be clearer. But beyond that, she's left Deja on her own. Deja clears her throat again.

"Teachers, Mr. Brown, and students of Carver Elementary School, my name is Deja—"

"Everyone already knows your name," Nikki interrupts.

"We're still supposed to introduce ourselves," Deja says. She continues, *". . . and I am running for student body president of Carver Elementary School."*

Nikki interrupts again. "I think you're saying Carver Elementary School too many times."

"I only said it twice."

"Well, it's too close together."

"I don't think so," Deja protests.

"Remember, I'm your campaign manager."

"So? You're not my boss."

"Well, you shouldn't have asked me to be your campaign manager if you're not even going to listen to me."

"Do you want to hear it or not?" Deja asks.

"I guess so," Nikki says, but she starts working on her lanyard again and barely looks up as Deja gives her speech. When she finishes, Nikki doesn't even act like she knows Deja has finished.

"What do you think?" Deja presses.

"It's okay."

"Is that all you have to say?"

"I didn't think you really wanted my opinion," Nikki replies.

"Well you're my campaign manager, aren't you?"

Nikki just shrugs and shakes her head. "I think you made too many promises."

"I have to promise stuff," Deja says. "Otherwise people might not vote for me."

"But, Deja . . ." Nikki begins, "more field trips for every class? How are you going to do that?"

"I don't know. I'll figure it out." Deja is sorry she even asked Nikki for her opinion. In fact, Deja doesn't know what Nikki has even done in her role as campaign manager except ask a few kids some questions. She didn't help with the posters, just because she was sulking. Just because Deja told Ms. Shelby something that could save Nikki's life.

"I don't think you will, Deja. I think you're just going to say it without figuring it out."

"No, I'm going to figure it out." Deja looks down at her cards.

"And longer recess?" Nikki says in a tone that shows she might be just getting started. "You can't do that."

"I can ask . . ."

"And, come on, fried chicken for lunch? When have we ever had fried chicken for lunch?"

"When are you not going to criticize so much?" Deja counters.

"Well, you asked my opinion."

"Your opinion is not very helpful."

"But remember, I'm your campaign manager."

"Well," Deja says, "a good campaign manager would have helped me with my posters."

"A good friend would have not been a tattletale." Nikki stands up.

"I told Ms. Shelby to save your life," Deja says, knowing she's exaggerating.

"No, you just wanted to be Miss Goody-Good, so Ms. Shelby would think you're so *mature!*" With that, Nikki turns and stomps up the steps into her house, slamming the front door behind her.

Deja stands there, frozen. Nikki knows her so well.

On Monday, Nikki remains cool. She has little to say on their walks to and from school and heads immediately to the handball court when Room Ten is let out for morning and lunch recess. When Deja asks her questions, she answers with as few words as possible. Deja decides to ignore this. Nikki has acted this way before. Eventually, she will forget why she's angry and things will go back to normal. Deja will just wait it out. Plus, when she's elected student body president of Carver Elementary, Nikki will be happy to be her best friend.

Tuesday, speech day, comes quickly. Deja can barely sit still, for two reasons. First, she is wearing the beautiful new lavender sweater that Auntie bought her. It's a little itchy, but it's the same color as the blossoms on the jacaranda tree that grows in front of a house on her street. Second, any minute a helper is going to come to Room Ten and pick her up. She will be taken to the auditorium to wait backstage for the assembly to start.

Assembly days are always good days because lots of work gets missed. Deja looks down at her open Sustained Silent Reading book and wonders why she chose one with so many pages. It's so boring, yet she's going to be stuck with it for another week because Ms. Shelby makes them keep the books they check out of the classroom library for two weeks. Nikki must have a great book. She looks as if she's really reading. Finally, there's a light rap on the door and one of the fifth grade helpers enters with a note for Ms. Shelby. Ms. Shelby reads it, nods, then smiles at Deja. "You're wanted in the auditorium, Deja."

All of the other candidates are already sitting in chairs lined up onstage when Deja enters. The last chair in the row is empty. It's her chair. She swallows hard and scratches an itchy spot just under the neck of her sweater. She suddenly feels hot.

"Oh, Deja," Mr. Willis says. He's the fifth grade teacher. "Come on up and take your seat."

The walk down the center aisle seems to take forever. She feels all eyes on her until she settles in her chair. Mr. Brown is fooling with the microphone onstage. He repeats, "Testing, testing, testing . . ." until his voice finally booms across the auditorium, making Deja jump. She feels her heart beat faster and, it seems, louder, too. She wonders if anyone can hear it. Surprisingly, her mouth feels dry, and the itchy spot just under her collar has now spread down her arms and across her back.

The auditorium doors open then, and in file the kindergarten classes. They take the front rows. Right behind them are the first- and second-graders. By the time the third-graders come in, the room is buzzing with anticipation. She can barely make out her own class. She can't even see Nikki. She'd feel better if she could see Nikki, even though Nikki's still being cool to her. In the car that morning (Nikki's mom had taken them to school), she'd kept her face turned toward her window and didn't speak to Deja. The fourth and fifth grade classes file in, and by the time they take their seats they are just a dim blur. Deja can't focus on the students in the crowd, but she can hear their rustling and their excited voices.

Mr. Brown takes the center of the stage and raises his hand with his five fingers spread out. "Five!" he says and looks around, waiting until most of the auditorium catches on.

"Five!" they repeat with their hands held up.

"Four!" he says, and looks around until they repeat what he says.

By the time he gets to three, the auditorium is perfectly quiet.

"That's better," he says. Then he gives a long

talk—at least it seems long to Deja—about auditorium behavior, which is different from playground behavior. He reminds them how important the day is and how hard the candidates have worked and how worthy they are to represent their classes. A lot of what he is saying doesn't sound all the way true. Deja looks down the row of seated students onstage. Gregory Johnson is sitting up straight and confident. Lashonda is yawning, and Paula is shuffling her feet. Sheena is playing with the ball barrette at the end of her braid, and Arthur is slouched, showing poor posture. The other fourth-grader is biting her thumbnail. But Deja supposes they are just as worthy as anyone else. She takes a big breath and slips her hand behind her back. She's able to scratch on the back of her neck just under her sweater. For a second, it feels better.

Suddenly, she hears her name. Mr. Brown is looking down the row at her with a big grin on his face. He's calling her up. She'd thought it would start the other way around, with her going last. But she's first.

Slowly, Deja gets up. Slowly, she walks to the microphone, which Mr. Brown is lowering to her height. This is it. She has her index cards clutched in her hand. She hasn't looked at them since that morning before school. She's a little panicked to see that they aren't in order. Where's the one with her introduction? She shuffles through them quickly, and they spill out of her hands. Laughter spreads across the auditorium.

"Excuse me?" Mr. Brown says in a booming voice.

It stops as suddenly as it started, but it leaves Deja feeling even more jittery.

"My name is Deja," she says. Mr. Willis rushes over and adjusts the microphone just as she's saying, "and I'm running for student body president of Carver Elementary." Her voice suddenly booms out in the middle of her sentence, startling her. She stops and looks at her cards. They seem as if they're covered with scribble. She can't make out one word.

She blurts out all of the things she'll do for the school if they elect her. Nikki was right. All her promises suddenly sound silly. They're just promises, with no thought behind them. She wishes she had something else to say, but she can't remember anything else, not even her closing. She just says thank you and takes her seat, feeling a tiny bit relieved that it is over.

Arthur is next and he is not much better. He basically lists all the reasons people should vote

for him. He sounds scared and unconvincing. Sheena holds her speech, written on a piece of notebook paper with torn holes, right in front of her face. She keeps stumbling over her own handwriting. Deja wants to laugh, but she suppresses it. Lashonda and the other fourth-grader wrote theirs kind of like poems. *Lashonda's is better,* Deja thinks. It's even funny.

Paula, from Mr. Hick's fifth grade, simply reads her speech like Sheena. But it sounds as if it was written by someone way older. Deja thinks Paula's mother probably wrote it because it it has a lot of big words that Paula can't pronounce. Deja really wants to laugh now. But she knows that would look bad, so she bites her tongue. Gregory Johnson does his in a kind of interesting way. After he introduces himself to the audience, they cheer. He then answers questions about what he will do as student body president from a question box he'd placed on a little table just inside the entrance to the school building. Deja wonders why she didn't think of that. She can feel everyone's total attention as he answers each question smoothly and with a big, confident smile. He even has on a shirt and tie. He already looks like a student body president.

When he's finished there are cheers and loud,

enthusiastic applause, which is more than the polite response Deja got. He takes his seat and Mr. Brown steps forward, clapping as he approaches the lowered microphone. He bends toward it to give his usual end-of-assembly talk about how to exit the auditorium in an orderly way. The candidates remain in their chairs onstage until everyone leaves. Then Mr. Willis dismisses them to their classrooms. Deja leaves the stage feeling she could have done better. She wishes she had another chance.

As soon as Deja enters the classroom, Ms. Shelby leads the students in applause for their classmate. "I know we're all excited about the election and the announcement of the results on Friday morning."

Some kids glance over at Deja; some don't even look like they're paying attention. Nikki gives her a tiny smile.

9

Last-Ditch Efforts

"Y ou did good, Deja," Nikki says as they walk home. Nikki is no longer giving her the silent treatment. *She must be feeling sorry for me,* Deja thinks. Why else would she suddenly act nice? "You could win," Nikki adds.

Deja doesn't say anything. She wants to believe it. But she can't. Gregory Johnson's speech was too good and he's so popular. She doesn't stand a chance. That's what she repeats to herself all the way home: *I don't stand a chance.*

She's still thinking this when Auntie Dee looks over at her across the dinner table and says, "How was your speech?"

"It was okay." Deja looks down at her food—

vegetarian lasagna—and pushes the carrots to the side. She'll get to them later. "Some of the other kids' speeches were better. Except Arthur's from Mr. Beaumont's class and Sheena's from Mrs. Miller's class. They were pretty bad. And this other girl read hers and couldn't even pronounce all the words."

"Do you understand why I wanted you to do it on your own without a lot of help from me?" Auntie Dee launches into her self-esteem talk—how true self-esteem comes out of one's own behavior and decisions and personal responsibility. Which means it's sometimes best if she lets Deja do things on her own, and blah, blah, blah. Deja still really wishes Auntie had written her speech for her. She takes a bite of whole wheat pasta. She chews and chews. It's more rubbery than the nice, soft, white kind that Nikki's mother serves.

"So, what happened?" Auntie asks.

"I forgot most of my speech and my promises sounded dumb."

Auntie chuckles and says, "It's not the end of the world."

"And now Lashonda or Gregory Johnson is probably going to win."

"What grades are they in?" Auntie asks.

"Fourth and fifth."

"Hmm," Auntie says. "Aren't there just two fourth grades and two fifth grades?"

"Yeah," says Deja.

"And then aren't there three third grades?"

"Yeah . . ." Deja wonders what Auntie is getting at.

"Maybe the lower grades will vote for you."

"Or Sheena or Arthur," Deja says.

"Just don't give up yet."

Deja has just about given up, despite Auntie Dee's pep talk. But then an idea comes to her in the middle of the night. Something has been missing from her campaign. Stuff! Giveaways! Like campaign buttons! If only she had campaign buttons. She needs lots and lots of them—enough for the two first grades (kindergarten isn't voting), the two second grades, and the three third grades. One hundred and forty buttons! How is she going to get one hundred and forty buttons? How much would that even cost? She thinks and thinks so much, it's hard to get back to sleep.

"You don't even know how to make campaign buttons," Nikki says on the way to school the next day.

"Well, what else can I do? I've got to do something."

Nikki's face lights up. "I know! Why don't you make cookies with icing that says 'Vote for Deja'?"

It takes a moment for Nikki's idea to register. Deja thinks of the candy rule. "I don't know if we'll be able to give out cookies, since we can't give out candy."

"Cookies aren't candy," Nikki says. "It's the same as when someone has a birthday and their mom brings cupcakes. It's exactly the same."

"I betcha we're the only ones thinking of this," Deja says, her eyes getting bigger and bigger with excitement.

"How can we give them out?"

"I bet Ms. Shelby will let us pass them out—if it's after lunch, maybe close to the end of the day, and all our work is done."

The more Deja thinks of this plan, the more everything seems to come together. They'll have to get permission right away. Then they'll have to get Auntie or Nikki's mom to buy the ingredients, and then they'll have to make the cookies. The vote is on Friday, so they'll have to hand out the cookies tomorrow. The memory of their delicious taste will still be fresh when the little kids cast their vote.

A big grin spreads across Deja's face as she

thinks of all the votes she's bound to get. "This is going to work!" she exclaims.

Ms. Shelby listens politely to their proposal. Perhaps she's thinking of all the times some birthday kid from another class delivered a piece of birthday cake to her and the other teachers. *This is kind of the same,* Deja thinks, *only they're cookies.*

"Let me check with Mr. Brown," Ms. Shelby says finally, "and I'll let you know tomorrow."

Deja stands there a moment, thinking past Ms. Shelby's words. They can't wait for permission tomorrow. They'll have to make the cookies without knowing. They'll have to get those big, fat refrigerator dough things—a lot of them. The ones where you only have to slice the dough. And those tubes of icing, the kind you write with. Lots of those. Auntie Dee will have to go to the store as soon as possible because they have to get started tonight.

But when Deja gets home and tells her plans to Auntie, who's on the treadmill, she pulls out one of her earphones and says skeptically, "You want to do *what?*"

"I need to make cookies so I can pass them out tomorrow. Auntie, I need you to go to the

store and get those refrigerator dough things."

Auntie Dee turns off the treadmill. "How many cookies do you have to make?"

"One hundred and forty," Deja says in a small voice, hoping that will make it go over better.

"One hundred and forty! And you tell me this *now?*"

"Puhleeze, Auntie. This is my last chance before the election on Friday. Puhleeze . . ."

Deja is careful not to put too much whine in her voice. She doesn't want to annoy Auntie Dee so much that she'll say no.

"Let me tell you something, Miss Priss. I'm going to show you how to make one batch and then you're on your own. Am I clear?"

"Yes, Auntie, you're clear."

Auntie Dee's lesson on preheating the oven and oven safety and how to use a potholder and how to use the icing tubes to write takes forever. Nikki is showing more patience than Deja. She sits at the table, listening politely. When the first batch of cookies comes out of the oven, Deja paces the floor as they cool. She keeps touching them with the knuckle of her forefinger to see if they're ready for the icing.

Luckily, Nikki's mom has let them use her oven as well. She brings two batches over as soon as they have cooled. In the first go-around, Nikki and Deja have forty-eight cookies to decorate with VOTE 4 DEJA! Auntie shows them how, and then lets them start writing on their own.

Of course, it's harder than it seems. Nikki's better at writing with icing than Deja is, and her cookies look much better. Until she gets the hang of it, Deja's letters are either too squished or too big. But because there are extra cookies, they just eat the ones she's messed up.

It isn't long before Nikki is flopping down in a

kitchen chair and saying, "My hand's tired. I need to rest."

"My hand's tired, too, but we still have thirty-one more cookies to do."

Auntie peeks in just then to remind them that bedtime is right around the corner.

Deja and Nikki sigh heavily at the same time.

Then, Auntie says the most wonderful thing that Deja has heard during her whole campaign: "Don't worry, I'll finish up."

Deja smiles happily and high-fives Nikki, just as Nikki is turning to high-five her.

Auntie has put the cookies in shoeboxes. They sit on Nikki's and Deja's laps as she drives them to school. "I'll talk to Ms. Shelby, and what she says goes. If we have to take the cookies back home, we'll just put them in the freezer." Deja lifts up a shoebox lid. Auntie put the cookies in the refrigerator overnight and now the icing is nice and hard. She's layered them between sheets of wax paper. Deja is quite proud of her cookies. She can't wait to give them out. *If* she can give them out.

"You two go get in line," Auntie says, parking a little bit down the street from the school and taking the boxes from Nikki and Deja. "I'll go talk to Ms. Shelby."

The girls head to the Room Ten line and before they know it, Auntie is walking toward them empty-handed, giving them the thumbs-up. Ms. Shelby must have said yes!

All day, Deja watches the clock, waiting for the moment when Ms. Shelby gives them permission to get up out of their seats, gather their boxes of cookies, and leave all of their classmates behind. At least the afternoon is partly taken up with a film on California Native Americans, which makes the time go faster.

Finally, after math, after social studies, and after the film, Ms. Shelby tells them that they may pass out the VOTE 4 DEJA! cookies. Again, Deja has butterflies in her stomach—this time, from anticipation. This whole election has made her stomach topsy-turvy.

The best part of knocking on classroom doors and explaining quietly to the teacher why she's there is knowing that all eyes are eagerly on her and her boxes of cookies. She wonders if Nikki is experiencing the same thing. Nikki's taking the other two third grades and their own class. Deja's taking the two first and second grades.

"Look with your eyes, not your hands," Mrs.

Mumford tells her second-graders as Deja passes the cookies around. Everyone is eager to get their little hands in the box to extract what they decide is the biggest cookie. Deja loves watching their faces as they read VOTE 4 DEJA! She loves hearing them say it out loud as they read.

As she leaves the first grades, she thinks her plan might work. "Don't forget to vote for me," she has said with each cookie she's handed out. This has been the best day of the entire election.

"I think I'm going to win," Deja says to Nikki on their way home.

"I think you are, too," Nikki agrees.

Deja has managed to save two cookies that would have gone to two kids who were absent. She pulls them out of her book bag and hands one to Nikki. Somehow, because the cookies are the key thing that's going to get her elected, they taste extra good. She smiles happily all the way home.

But the next day, as she and Nikki enter the schoolyard, Deja stops short. There are VOTE FOR GREG! buttons everywhere. Almost every kid Deja sees has a big, glittery VOTE FOR GREG! button pinned to their shirt or blouse. One kid has it pinned to his cap, which he's not supposed to be wearing, anyway. Deja stands frozen in place. She can't believe her eyes.

"Where did they get those?" Nikki exclaims.

"Gregory Johnson must have given them out."

Just then, one of the first-graders runs by, holding up a button and calling out to Nikki and Deja, "Gregory Johnson is giving these away—for free! You should go get one!"

Ayanna joins them, happy, it seems, to bring them up to speed. "He's been passing them out since he got here—to everybody!"

Deja is dumbfounded. She opens her mouth to speak, but nothing comes out.

Nikki speaks for her. "Uh-oh."

That's just what Deja is thinking. *Uh-oh*.

Then Nikki shakes her head sadly. "I bet they forgot all about your cookies, Deja."

Deja knows she's right, but she just can't think of anything to say.

10

When All Is Said and Done

The voting takes place in the classrooms after morning recess. There's a special box for each classroom where students will place their ballots. The boxes will then be taken to the office where the votes will be counted, and Mr. Brown will announce the winner after lunch recess. Deja tries to read her classmates' faces as they mark their ballots, fold them, and walk to the special box to drop them in.

What will be will be, she thinks. She's heard Auntie say that before. A lot of times.

The PA system begins to crackle right in the middle of *The Whipping Boy*. Deja gasps— softly, so she doesn't think anyone has heard. Ms. Shelby stops reading and holds up her hand for silence. Nikki looks over at Deja and her eyes are big like saucers. That just makes Deja more nervous.

Then they hear Mr. Brown's official-sounding voice:

"Good afternoon, students of Carver Elementary School. This is your principal. I know we've had lots of excitement these last two weeks with our first school-wide election. And, I'm sure we're all anxious to hear who is going to be our first student body president."

Deja wonders how long he's going to talk without really saying anything. Antonia, who Deja hasn't even paid that much attention to today, looks over at her. Ayanna and ChiChi turn around in their seats to look at her, too. Ms. Shelby smiles encouragingly. Mr. Brown drones on.

Then, finally, he announces it. *"Our new student body president is Gregory Johnson."*

The cheers and hollers from the fifth grade classrooms can be heard all the way down the hall. Room Ten is silent. Surprisingly, Antonia doesn't smirk at Deja, but sits facing straight ahead. Nikki gives Deja a sympathetic look, and Ms. Shelby walks over and puts her hand on

Deja's shoulder. "You did a great job, Deja. So don't be discouraged. There was only going to be one winner. Maybe next year."

Deja nods slowly and swallows hard. She doesn't say anything because she's afraid that her voice will be shaky.

"You know what we're going to do, class?" Ms. Shelby says. She walks over to her desk and picks up a small stack of yellow construction paper. "I'd planned to have you make congratulations cards for whoever won. So, we're going to make congratulations cards for Gregory Johnson." She nods and smiles and raises her eyebrows like she's really happy.

Ms. Shelby places a piece of yellow construction paper on Deja's desk and Deja looks down at it blankly. She has no idea what she will write. After a few moments, she sighs and lifts her pencil. Maybe stuff will come to her after she writes the word *Congratulations.*

Congratulations Gregory Johnson. I can't say I'm real happy that you won over me. I think you won because your one of the big kids and you gave out all those buttons that people can put on and keep. And maybe people think you can do a better job. But I can to even tho I'm in third grade.

But I say congratulations anyway. I hope you do a good job and make our school famous and make all the kids good kids and make it so people want to come to Carver Elementary. I hope you stop kids from fighting and make them do there homework and be nice and respect all the teachers like they should. Thats what I was going to do. Maybe it was going to be hard. But I was going to try anyway. So thats all I got to say. So congratulations again.

Deja sighs again and draws a rainbow on the front. It's what she really knows how to draw best.

"What were the results?" Auntie Dee asks, opening the door before Deja can even take out her key.

"Gregory Johnson," Deja says flatly. She turns to wave goodbye to Nikki, who is opening the door to her own house.

"Oh . . . I'm sorry," Auntie says with the kind of half smile that looks like it's meant to show sympathy. "What can I do?"

Deja shrugs.

"You want to go out for pizza?" They almost never go out for pizza.

Deja shrugs again.

But Auntie seems to know what those shrugs mean. "Go get Nikki," she says. "We're going for pizza." She turns to pick up the telephone to call Nikki's mother. "I'm sure her parents will appreciate an evening alone," Auntie Dee says.

Later, in the car on their way to the pizza place, Nikki nudges Deja. Deja looks down. Nikki is holding a hot cinnamon sucker. "You had this left in your candy bag."

"I'm going to run next year," Deja repeats resolutely, and holds out her sucker to Nikki so that she can share in its yumminess. "And I betcha I'll win."